Murder
Conspiracy

MACK
JENKINS

TABLE OF CONTENT

Chapter 1

Caution tapes littered around the crime scene, and uniformed men surrounded the area, preventing passersby from getting close. The low murmur of police radios filled the air, making up the background noise in the scenery. Their sirens resonated through the air. From afar, onlookers craned their necks to get a view of the cause of the commotion.

Detectives Shawn Parker and Diana Maxwell arrived at the scene, their presence commanding attention as they flashed their ID cards to bypass the barricade of uniformed officers.

Shawn's eyes scanned the area, taking in the grim picture before him. The lifeless body lay sprawled on the floor, a pool of crimson spreading around it. It was a gruesome sight, but the detectives remained focused, their minds honed to dissect the clues hidden within the gruesome scene.

With practiced precision, they approached the body. Diana crouched down and carefully examined the victim's back. "From the state of the wounds," she began, her voice steady despite the grisly sight, "it looks like the assailant attacked from behind." She glanced at Shawn, her eyes reflecting concern. As if on cue, they both dipped their hands into their pockets, slipping out their white gloves to prevent contaminating the crime scene with their fingerprints.

A characteristic slap sound met their ears as they pulled on the vinyl gloves. "He sustained multiple blows to the occipital region of his head, and a few on his temples. He was probably struck from behind, and when he turned around, the assailant continued to strike, hitting harder on his temples." Diana's voice was monotonous and devoid of emotions as she spoke. It was a drill they were well acquainted with.

"And from the direction the body is facing, he probably fell after the fatal hits on his temples. It seems he was jogging towards the streets, away from the alley over there," Shawn responded, pointing. "A dark alley is a perfect spot for a criminal to hide and carry out this murder when the victim least expects it," he added.

Diana smiled, her lips curling into a wicked grin. "Well well well, look at the surprise the killer left for us," she said, pointing with her nose at a blood-stained meat mallet, the silver object glistening under the morning sun, as if begging to be noticed.

"They probably dropped it in the heat of the moment and scurried away."

Diana nodded in agreement and reached into her back pocket, pulling out a portable GoPro camera and taking pictures of the crime scene from various angles. Carefully, she picked up the mallet, her gloved hands stained with blood. She sealed it in a protective evidence bag, her movements deliberate and focused. Shawn also retrieved some items like the victim's wallet and phone. He went through the wallet, retrieving an ID card.

"Jefferson Crawford," he mouthed as he read the name on the driver's license out loud. Shawn continued to search the crime scene for any additional clues. He moved methodically from one corner to the next, carefully examining his surroundings as his mind raced to put the pieces of the puzzle together. Knowing that every second could be vital in catching the offender, it was a race against time.

Shawn and Diana were a lethal combo; they had never lost a case before, which quickly boosted their careers even at their young age. With them on a case, the criminal was better off turning themselves in because the duo was relentless, sharp, and ruthless.

Their highly analytical minds were already in full gear as they considered every move, every viewpoint, and every eventuality that might have occurred.

"I think that's about it," Diana said to the paramedics, allowing them to wrap the body and transport it to the lab for an autopsy. As they walked back to the car, she and Shawn exchanged looks. "We need to learn more about this Jefferson person." Shawn nodded, agreeing with her.

*****

Victoria's home was filled with an oppressive silence, punctuated only by her anguished wails and the soft sobbing of her two children, Tristan and Taylor.

The news of Jefferson's untimely death shattered the family, leaving them in the throes of a devastating emotional breakdown. Victoria sat on the couch, her body trembling with grief, tears streaming down her face uncontrollably. "Why him? Why?" she muttered, her body shivering as more tears streamed down. The police had arrived earlier in the morning to break the news, asking some basic questions before leaving.

A knock on the door interrupted their sorrowful moment. Taylor, eyes red and swollen from crying, stood up to open the door. Detectives Shawn Parker and Diana Maxwell stood outside, their faces bearing expressions of empathy mixed with professionalism.

Flashing their ID cards, they entered the house, casting a glance at Victoria's inconsolable state. Tristan, noticing the detectives' presence, excused himself from the grieving scene and approached them. His face was puffy, evidence of the raw emotions he had been battling.

Shawn looked down at Tristan, his voice gentle as he spoke, "Tristan, we need to ask you a few questions about what happened to Jefferson. We're here to find out the truth and bring justice to your family."

Tristan nodded, his voice thick with emotion as he responded, "Of course, Detective. Anything to help find out who did this to him." He led the detectives away to a quieter corner of the house, leaving Taylor to comfort their devastated mother.

Taylor moved closer to Victoria, wrapping her arms around her mother's trembling frame. She held her tightly, rubbing her back soothingly, her voice a tender whisper. "It's going to be okay, Mom. We'll get through this together. Tristan is talking to the detectives. They'll help us find out who did this to Jefferson."

Victoria's sobs subsided slightly, and she looked up at Taylor with bloodshot eyes filled with grief. Her voice cracked as she choked out words between hushed sobs, "I can't believe he's gone, Taylor. He was everything to us. How am I supposed to go on without him?"

"You still have us mom, everything will be okay. Just calm down," she said in a soothing tone.

On the other side of the room, Tristan was being interviewed. "Where was everyone on the night of the murder?"

He cleared his throat, "they were all here, sleeping. I was at my girlfriend Natalie's house; I returned this morning and we got the news of his death this morning." Diana nodded, scribbling something in her notepad.

"When was the last time you guys saw Jefferson?"

"Yesterday actually, he was here in the afternoon before he left."

Victoria's stifled sobs met their ears as she cried on Taylor's shoulders. "I should've never argued with him," she cried, filled with grief. Shawn raised an eyebrow, turning to face her.

"I'm sorry, did you say argue?"

"She's not in the state to talk. Please don't stress her," Taylor responded.

"No, it's okay baby. Yes, we had an argument when he came over in the afternoon."

Shawn turned to face Tristan, wondering why he hadn't told him about this.

"The kids weren't home," Victoria quickly added.

Shawn nodded slowly.

"What was this argument about, if you don't mind my asking?"

"Money issues, nothing much. He left in annoyance. I wish I knew, I wish we made up," she said, breaking into more sobs.

"It's not your fault. You had no idea," Diana, who'd been quiet since, finally spoke. "We'll get to the bottom of this," she said, making a promise more to herself than to Victoria.

After that, Diana and Shawn headed back to their office. They alighted from the car and entered the office of the coroner, their footsteps echoing off the sterile walls. The weight of the case rested heavily on their shoulders; they were eager to uncover any new insights that the autopsy results might provide. They approached the coroner's desk with brisk steps.

"Dr. Philip, do you have the results of Jefferson's autopsy?" Diana inquired, her arm folded against her chest.

The coroner nodded, reaching for the file on his desk. He opened it and began to read from the report. His voice was clinical but compassionate. "The cause of death, as determined by the extensive cranial fractures, was a series of repeated blows to the skull. We counted approximately ten distinct impacts."

Shawn and Diana shared a knowing look. The brutality of the attack and the deliberate nature of the blows showed a vicious intent. It was a stark confirmation that this was no crime of randomness but a meticulously planned act of violence.

Diana's voice cut through the tense silence as she continued analyzing the findings. "Were there any fingerprints found on the body or the meat mallet?"

The coroner shook his head, disappointment etched on his face. "No, Detective. There were no discernible fingerprints present. It seems the killer took precautions to avoid leaving any identifiable marks."

Shawn clenched his jaw, his mind racing to connect the dots. The absence of fingerprints suggested the killer had likely worn gloves, leaving no trace behind. It was a calculated move, one that spoke volumes about their level of preparation and awareness.

Diana's eyes narrowed as another piece of the puzzle fell into place. "What about the meat mallet? Did you find anything significant?"

The coroner adjusted his glasses before responding. "Interestingly, the meat mallet was relatively new, with minimal signs of wear and tear. It appeared to have been recently purchased or acquired."

Shawn and Diana locked eyes, a silent understanding passing between them. This was not a random item found at the scene; it was deliberately chosen. The killer had specifically acquired a new meat mallet, likely to avoid leaving any traces that might connect them to the crime.

Diana spoke with conviction, her voice laced with determination. "This was a premeditated murder. The killer not only planned the attack but also made efforts to conceal their identity. It's clear they had a connection to Jefferson. They knew him."

Shawn nodded in agreement, his mind already racing with the possibilities. Every piece of evidence pointed to a calculated killer, someone who had carefully plotted their actions and knew enough about Jefferson to carry out such a brutal act.

Shawn and Diana created a flowchart, trying to connect Jefferson to people they knew he knew. "We have to go to that apartment complex he lived in; he has neighbors that may help us. Even his apartment might have clues."

****

Shawn and Diana stood outside the apartment complex where Jefferson had lived, their gazes scanning the surroundings as they prepared to dive deeper into their investigation. The air tingled with anticipation as they approached the first neighbor's door.

They knocked on the door, and after a moment, it swung open to reveal a middle-aged man named Paul. He looked at the detectives with furrowed brows, recognizing their authority as they flashed their ID cards.

"Good afternoon, sir," Diana began, her tone polite, "We're investigating the unfortunate demise of Jefferson. We were wondering if you might have any information that could help us."

Paul nodded and invited them inside, his expression somber. "I didn't know Jefferson too well, but I'll share what I can. Please come in."

They settled into Paul's living room, Shawn and Diana leaning forward attentively as Paul recounted what he knew. He mentioned seeing Jefferson having a conversation with someone on the streets the evening of his death. The individuals involved didn't appear to be having a friendly discussion, raising suspicions in Paul's mind.

"Did you recognize the person Jefferson was talking to?" Shawn asked.

"Yeah, it was this guy named Eric. He used to come around occasionally. I didn't know him well, but there were rumors that he was involved in some illegal activities. Jefferson never really seemed too happy to see him when he came by. It could be worth looking into."

Diana jotted down notes, her mind already forming connections. "Do you have any information about Jefferson's acquaintances? Anyone who might be relevant to our investigation?"

Paul pondered for a moment before responding. "Apart from Eric, not really."

Shawn's eyes gleamed with renewed interest. "Thank you, sir. Your information is valuable. We'll definitely follow up on that lead."

Returning to Jefferson's apartment, Shawn paused, contemplating their next move. The lack of leads within his living space left them with a pressing need to uncover more about the man himself. The time had come to delve deeper into Jefferson's background, searching for clues that might reveal his secrets and unearth potential motives for his murder.

Shawn turned to Diana, determination etched on his face. "We need to find out more about Jefferson. Let's gather all the information we can about his personal life, his relationships, and his past. We need to understand who he was and what might have led to his tragic end."

Time flew by as they searched his house, leaving no stone unturned. They ended up finding some sticks of weed scattered around his house in different locations. "Too bad you can't arrest the dead," Diana joked, flicking one into the dustbin.

"Alright, nothing much here. We just found out he smoked and was very untidy," Shawn said.

"Maybe that Eric guy Paul mentioned is his weed supplier."

Shawn arched his eyebrow. "Well, that'd be illegal, but that's not our main focus. Our main goal now is uncovering the killer."

Diana leaned against a table as she responded. "A drug dealer could have several motivations for killing someone, a disagreement, a debt... I mean we've handled cases like this before."

"Let's interrogate Eric."

*****

Shawn sat behind his desk in his office. He had just finished going through the details on Eric. As Shawn perused Eric's record, he discovered a troubled past; he was an ex-convict, jailed for various crimes, including drug trafficking, indicating a propensity for illegal activities.

Just as he was deep in thought, the office door creaked open, and Eric stepped inside. Shawn eyed him carefully, his trained gaze evaluating every nuance of Eric's demeanor. He saw a man with hardened features, a hint of caution in his eyes. Shawn motioned for Eric to take a seat, his expression one of calm authority.

"Good afternoon, Eric," Shawn began, his voice measured but assertive. "I'll cut straight to the point: where were you in the evening of July 8th?"

Eric smiled. "The night my pal Jefferson was murdered? I went over to talk to him before heading to the strip club," he said with a confident grin.

"Would you mind sharing what you discussed with Jefferson?"

For a brief while, Eric's gaze darted around the room as uncertainty appeared on his face. His posture was stiff as he sat down on the chair after slowly exhaling. "I had nothing to do with Jefferson's death, Detective. I swear it! We were only speaking."

Shawn leaned forward, his voice firm. "Eric, I understand you might be hesitant to trust the police, given your past. But we're here to find the truth. If there's something you know, something that could help us solve this case, now is the time to come forward."

Shawn's gaze met Eric's as his jaw tightened. "Detective, I've made up for my previous faults. I've changed my way of life. But that doesn't imply I have faith in you folks to handle my private matters. I had my reasons for speaking with Jefferson that evening, and I won't share them with you."

Even though Shawn was deeply frustrated, he managed to remain calm. He knew that exerting too much pressure might make Eric entirely close up. Instead, he changed his strategy and spoke sympathetically. "Eric, I recognize your worries. But now is your chance to show that you had nothing to do with the murder of Jefferson. Please tell me all about this discussion. It might contain a tip that can help us find the true murderer."

Eric's eyes briefly filled with doubt as his gaze faltered. He appeared conflicted, split between the need to clear his name and the urge to protect himself. "I won't say anything. It's a personal matter, and I won't jeopardize my safety for something I didn't do. You'll need to take a different path."

"Jeopardize? So, you are doing something illegal then?"

Eric swallowed the lump forming in his throat. "I have other engagements for today. Would that be all?" He asked.

"You never denied your involvement in illegal dealings Mr. Montgomery," Shawn said with a smile.

He shrugged, "maybe because I'm innocent," he said and turned away, walking towards the exit. Shawn wasn't satisfied.

Chapter 2

Tristan and Taylor sat on opposite sides of the bed, with Victoria slumped in the middle. The room felt heavy with an air of sadness as they waited for the doctor to conclude his assessment. His words hung in the silence, echoing the truth they had feared.

"I'm afraid Victoria's mute state is a result of severe depression," the doctor explained gently, his voice filled with compassion. "The trauma of losing Jefferson has deeply affected her. It's crucial to provide her with emotional support and encourage regular checkups. Therapy could be beneficial as well."

Tristan and Taylor listened intently, absorbing every word. They understood the gravity of their mother's condition. Thankfully, the doctor's professional advice offered a glimmer of hope amidst the despair that had consumed their lives.

Just as the doctor rose from his chair and prepared to leave, they heard a knock at the door. Tristan hesitated, uncertain about letting anyone else into their fragile world. But when he peered through the peephole and saw Shawn and Diana, he decided to grant them access.

Shawn and Diana entered. The room felt suddenly crowded as they exchanged glances with Tristan and Taylor, the gravity of the situation weighing heavily upon them all.

Shawn took a deep breath and addressed Tristan directly. "We've retrieved text messages from Jefferson's phone, and it seems that he had a history of violence. Why didn't anyone mention that he used to beat your mother?"

"We didn't think their personal lives were relevant to the case," Taylor said.

Shawn sighed, "Everything, absolutely everything, is relevant to this case; don't leave out any detail."

"Okay, we didn't know. We'll tell you everything from now on."

"As it stands, your refusal to divulge huge information like this makes your mom a suspect already; she has the perfect motivation. And you kids could be trying to cover her up for killing her abusive ex. That's why you omitted that detail."

"What does this have to do with anything? Are you suggesting that our mom could be the killer? That's absurd!" Tristan yelled.

Diana, too, seemed taken aback by Shawn's unexpected accusation. Her eyes shifted between the distraught family members and then back to her co-worker. "Shawn, I think that's a bit extreme. The woman is literally sitting there, lost in space. She's still mourning."

"She could be pretending," Shawn responded.

Tristan clenched his jaws. "I suggest you leave now."

As Shawn backed away, his gaze flickered to Taylor's face, catching a glimpse of the bruise on her lower jaw. He couldn't let it go unnoticed, his instincts as a detective urged him to question further.

"Taylor, you have a bruise on your jaw. What happened?" He asked, his voice laced with suspicion.

Taylor's eyes widened in surprise, her hand instinctively moving to touch the tender spot. She stumbled over her words, searching for an explanation. "Oh, um, I... I had something fall off my shelf. It hit me on the face by accident."

Tristan's confusion deepened as he looked at his sister, his protective instincts kicking in. He pulled her closer to him, inspecting her bruise. "When did it happen? Why didn't you tell me?"

"It happened just yesterday; I didn't think it was of any importance."

He turned to face Shawn. "Please leave. My mother doesn't need this stress."

"Just one last question and I promise we'll leave. You said you were with Natalie the night of the murder?" Dianna asked. Tristan nodded.

"Could you call her right now and confirm this to us? Don't let her know it's on speaker."

"Why would I call my girlfriend in front of everyone?"

"Because you have nothing to hide."

With a sigh, Tristan pulled out his phone and called her, putting the phone on loudspeaker.

"Hello? Tristan? What's up?"

"I'm good. Hey, um, where were you on Thursday?" Tristan asked.

She fell silent for a while. "Uh, I was home and you came over. Have you forgotten?" She asked with a chuckle. "Why?"

"I'll talk to you later, gotta go." He hung up, looking at them with an irritated expression. He watched as Shawn and Diana exited. Then he pulled his twin into a tight hug as the door closed, reassuring her that they would get through this.

*****

"Come out now," the text read as her phone buzzed. She checked to confirm her mother, Victoria, was in her room and that Tristan was sleeping soundly. Assured that her actions wouldn't disturb them, she quietly opened the door and slipped out into the night.

There, waiting for her, was David Harris—a charismatic young man known for his charm, yet also recognized as a felon within the neighborhood. Despite his checkered past, his handsome features and magnetic presence had drawn Taylor in. As they embraced, Shawn, hidden inside his car at a distance, observed their encounter with confusion lingering in his gaze. He was spying on the Greenes, hoping to uncover something.

Taylor's voice, filled with longing, broke the silence. "I've missed you so much, David. You've been away for too long."

David smiled, "I missed you too." They shared a tender but short kiss. Taylor's eyes flickered with regret as she spoke softly.

"I'm sorry for making you wait. Things have been difficult lately."

"It's okay. We have all the time now to make up for that. I'm back in town."

As their brief meeting came to an end, Shawn, parked nearby, watched David depart. His mind churned with questions, his detective instincts firing on all cylinders. He needed to dig deeper into David Harris's profile and his connection to the recent events surrounding Jefferson's death.

Driving back to the office, Shawn couldn't shake the nagging feeling that David's sudden reappearance in town was no coincidence. He turned his attention to the board, linking David to Eric. David used to be Eric's apprentice before he was jailed for stealing from Eric. He disappeared from the town after he was released from jail, only to show up at the same time that Jefferson was killed. This was definitely a significant connection, another piece of the puzzle.

The timeline of events overlapped. Shawn contemplated the possibilities, wondering if David had any involvement in the tragic event that had torn Victoria's world apart. There were still missing pieces, but the threads were beginning to weave together.

He picked up his phone, dialing Diana's number, eagerly waiting for her to pick up as his body twitched with excitement. Finally, the other line screeched.

"Hello, Diana? Sorry to bother you at this time. I just discovered something. Could you make it to the office now?"

"That's funny because I was just contemplating something as well. I have a new suspect with strong motivations," she replied, her voice matching his excitement.

"Then it's a date," he said, hanging up.

In barely 30 minutes, Diana walked into the office. "Did you speed here?" Shawn asked.

"100 miles per hour baby."

Shawn chuckled. "So, ladies first."

"I just discovered a new suspect, Lucas Greene. You see, I was doing some digging on personal info when I discovered that Victoria was divorced. She and Lucas didn't really have a great marriage, and guess what the interesting part is?

"What?" He asked.

"Lucas was an abusive man, and from my profiling, he seems to be a very self-centered, jealous, temperamental person. Nothing like an obsessed ex killing your partner."

Shawn sighed, analyzing the possibility. "That is a strong motivation I admit, but I'm suspecting David Harris."

"Who's David Harris?"

"He's a known felon, worked for Eric in the past, went to jail, left town, and came back around the time Jefferson was killed. Who's to say he wasn't Eric's machinery? Plus, he's Taylor's boyfriend, I think. I mean, they kissed."

She furrowed her brows. "How do you know all this?" She asked.

"I have my ways."

"So, who's a bigger suspect?"

"It's definitely Lucas," she replied.

"I think it's David," he countered.

"Wanna bet?" She said, sticking out her pinky with a mischievous grin.

"Okay, 50 bucks, " he says, locking fingers with her.

Chapter 3

Natalie sat on the couch in Tristan's house, her fingers anxiously twirling a lock of her hair. Her phone suddenly rang, startling her as she received the call she'd been expecting. Her expression turned pale as she answered her phone, her eyes widening with surprise. Tristan noticed her change in demeanor and concern flickered across his face.

"What's wrong, Natalie? Is everything alright?" he asked, his voice filled with worry.

Natalie hesitated for a moment, trying to find the right words. "They just called from the lab, Tristan. The doctor thinks I might be pregnant, but I need to go back for a proper test to confirm."

Tristan's face lit up with a mix of joy and excitement. He pulled Natalie into a tight embrace, his heart racing with anticipation. "That's amazing news, Natalie! We're going to have a baby!"

Just as the couple celebrated their joyous revelation, a knock resounded at the door. Tristan went to answer it, finding Shawn and Diana standing on the doorstep. Shawn's eyes flickered to Natalie, recognizing the emotions written across her face.

"Tristan, how is Victoria doing? Any improvement?" Shawn inquired, his voice filled with concern.

Tristan's expression darkened, and he shook his head with a heavy sigh. "No, Detective. There hasn't been any improvement. It's been really tough."

Just as the somber atmosphere settled, Taylor walked into the room, her presence bringing a renewed sense of energy. Natalie's eyes lit up as she turned to Taylor, unable to contain her excitement. "Taylor, guess what? I just found out that I might be pregnant. You're going to be an aunt soon!"

The news that a baby was possibly going to be born brought warmth to Taylor's heart. Her lips curled into a wide smile that wrinkled the corner of her eyes as she flashed her dentition. At least there was one ray of light piercing through the dark clouds looming over their family. "That's so great Natalie. Congratulations," she said.

Natalie smiled back in response.

Diana's interest was piqued as she listened to the conversation between Tristan and Natalie; they discussed possible baby names. Regardless of the good news the family was celebrating, there was still a murder case to solve. Diana turned her attention to Taylor and questioned her gently but persistently. "Taylor, can you describe the relationship between your mom's boyfriend and your father?"

Taylor hesitated for a moment before responding, her voice tinged with sadness. "To be honest, it was bad. None of them really liked the other. They even had a recent confrontation, and I remember my dad saying he'd kill Jefferson."

Diana's suspicions grew, and her mind raced to connect the dots. The volatile relationship between Lucas and Jefferson, combined with the escalating tensions, painted a picture of a possible motive.

Tristan's attention shifted to Taylor, his voice filled with concern. "Taylor, where are you coming from? You seem stressed."

Taylor's eyes darted nervously, her instinct to protect herself and keep her secrets held firm. "Oh, just from a friend's place," she replied, attempting to mask her unease.

Unbeknownst to Taylor, Shawn's trained eye caught the signs of deception. He couldn't understand why she was hiding her whereabouts nor the cause of her evident distress. The puzzle pieces continued to shift, forming a complex framework of interconnected lives, secrets, and potentially dangerous alliances. He was almost one hundred percent certain that she was with David.

*****

Shawn walked into the dimly lit interrogation room, his gaze fixed on David Harris. The air in the room seemed charged with tension as the two locked eyes. Shawn took a deep breath, his voice steady but firm.

"Why did you do it, David?" Shawn's question hung in the air, catching David off guard.

David's eyebrows furrowed in confusion. "Do what? I didn't kill Jefferson. I don't know what you're talking about."

Shawn leaned in, his eyes narrowing with suspicion. "But I never said you killed anyone. I only said why did you do *it*," Shawn repeated. "We have evidence linking you to Eric. It's possible he enlisted your help in killing Jefferson. Why did you come to town around the same time Jefferson was killed?"

David's eyes darted back and forth as he processed Shawn's words. He shook his head, a mix of frustration and disbelief crossing his face. "This is just a coincidence, Detective. I came back because I wanted to fix things with Taylor. That's all I care about."

Shawn's gaze intensified, searching for any signs of deception. He pressed on, his voice unwavering. "Fix things with Taylor? Did something happen between you two?"

David hesitated for a moment, his guard slipping. "Look, we had our issues. We broke up for a while. But I came back to make things right. I didn't harm Jefferson, and I have no interest in anything else except reconnecting with Taylor, especially after what happened since our last breakup.

Shawn's eyes narrowed further, sensing a vulnerability in David's words. He pushed a little further, his voice sharp and direct. "You hit Taylor, didn't you? During your last breakup," he said, taking a long shot.

David's face paled, his composure crumbling. He struggled to find words, caught off guard by the revelation. "I… I lost control, but I would never hurt her. I regret it deeply, and I was hoping to make amends."

Shawn's suspicions heightened, his mind processing the new information. The picture was starting to come together, and the pieces were falling into place.

Leaning back, Shawn studied David closely.

"Alright, that'll be all," Shawn finally broke the silence, getting on his feet. He felt uneasy as he walked out of the interrogation room, feeling the heat of David's stares on his back.

The next day, Shawn walked into the office, hanging his blazer on his chair. Diana followed behind him, wearing a fitted navy blue suit. She sighed as she retrieved her laptop from her bag, setting it up on her desk. "Another day has come and we have no new lead. We're being very sluggish Shawn," she said as she tapped away on her keyboard, signing into her computer.

"Oh, don't worry, I have a feeling the killer isn't going anywhere far any time soon."

She furrowed her eyebrows. "What if the killer isn't even any of our suspects? We have to look at it from that angle too, you know."

Shawn shrugged, "I know."

She narrowed her eyes on him, sensing that he was holding back some information, but she didn't bother to probe her partner any further. This wasn't her first rodeo with Shawn, and she trusted his intuition in matters like this. She opened the files she'd created for this case and began to inspect all the evidence once again, trying to draw a logical conclusion that could shed some new light on the case.

Just then, the telephone in the office rang, its slightly annoying repetitive buzz resonating through the air. Diana shot her head towards it and then back at Shawn. He extended his arm and reached for the handset.

"Hello?" He called. Silence fell for a few seconds before his eyes widened, making Diana inquisitive. He nodded, "Okay, we'll be on our way."

He jumped to his feet, retrieving his black blazer. "So, are you going to tell me what that was about?" She questioned.

Without stopping, he reached for the doorknob, yanking the door open as he made his way outside, with Diana following behind on her toes. "David's dead. He was murdered brutally on the streets. We have to get to the scene now."

Diana's features morphed into one of pure confusion as they made their way to the car.

They alighted from the car at almost the same time, quickening their pace as they rushed towards the crime scene, flashing their ID cards to prevent unnecessary delay. They came to a halt as they reached the scene, where they found the body covered in blood.

David Harris was lying flat on his back, the pink fleshy parts of his brain exposed due to his cracked skull. Diana's eyes landed on the blood-stained hammer lying conveniently beside the victim. "I'm sure it has no print," she said as she wore her vinyl gloves.

Shawn squinted his eyes at David's lifeless form, taking all the necessary evidence he could before the blaring sirens approached them. As the detectives made their way back to the car, Diana cleared her throat.

"Well, that's one suspect off the list," she remarked.

"So, who do you think did it?"

"Did what?"

"Killed Harris?"

She pondered on the question for a moment, "Well, seeing that a hammer, which is a very similar weapon to a meat mallet, was used, and the same killing pattern was employed, it's safe to say that it's most likely the same killer since there's a pattern of murder weapons, style, and time. He was most likely killed at night when the streets were lonely. Also, it has to be someone who has something against David. So, it's Eric."

A hint of dissatisfaction danced in his eyes as he considered the possibility. "Why Eric?"

"As revenge? I mean, wasn't it because of Eric's open threat that David left town?"

Shawn started the car, driving away from the sidewalk. His mind a battlefield of raging thoughts. He doesn't believe Eric did it.

Shawn and Diana stood on Victoria's doorstep, their expressions somber and heavy with news they silently wished not to deliver. They took a deep breath, mentally preparing themselves for the nature of the interaction that lay ahead. Shawn, ever vigilant, kept a watchful eye on Taylor as they entered the house, trying to gauge her reaction.

Tristan and Taylor were huddled together in the living room, their faces etched with concern as Shawn and Diana walked in. The room fell into a tense silence, the weight of their presence palpable. Shawn's gaze flickered between the twins, monitoring their reactions closely.

With a heavy sigh, Diana broke the news. "We have something to tell you all. David Harris is dead. He was found dead earlier today."

Taylor's face contorted with a mix of anguish and shock. Tears streamed down her cheeks as her voice trembled, choked with sorrow. The truth struck her like a devastating blow. Shawn's vigilance paid off as he noticed the genuine pain in her reaction.

Tristan, however, remained calm, his expression somber yet seemingly unsurprised by the news. He pulled Taylor close, offering her comfort, and whispered words of encouragement. "It's going to be okay, Taylor. You deserve better. He used to hurt you, remember? It's not worth it."

Diana and Shawn exchanged a knowing glance, their suspicions solidifying. Tristan had been aware of Taylor's involvement with David even before his return to town. Their shared understanding illuminated a dark truth—one that hinted at a cycle of abuse that Taylor had endured.

As the detectives prepared to leave, Shawn couldn't let go of his curiosity. He turned to Tristan, his voice gentle but probing. "Tristan, may I ask how you knew Taylor was seeing David?"

Tristan's gaze met Shawn's. He took a deep breath, gathering his thoughts before responding. "I knew about Taylor and David for some time now. But I only found out that he was back in town a few days ago when I saw Taylor crying after he hurt her."

Shawn nodded, his expression showing concern. His thoughts raced, making connections, and formulating a fresh notion. As the puzzle pieces came together, it became clear that Jefferson's murder had been the result of a perilous and dark path.

As they walked out of the house, they knew that this was a turning point in the investigation. David Harris was dead, so he definitely didn't do it. Shawn looked over his shoulders back at the house, a new idea forming in his mind. "So, Tristan knew the entire time," he muttered under his breath, catching Diana's attention.

She let out a sharp breath. "Let's just get the results of David's autopsy before drawing any conclusions."

Natalie decided she would spend the night at Tristan's place to support him. Taylor was mourning and Victoria was mute due to depression. She couldn't bear to let him handle it all alone.

"Thank you so much, Natalie. I feel calmer when you're here. Heaven knows who the killer is and who their next target is."

He pulled her into a tight side hug while rubbing Taylor's back.

Chapter 4

Dark circles had formed under Taylor's eyes as she sat on the dining table, staring into space. Tristan came out of his room, his backpack strap clutched tightly in his grip. He planted a small peck on his sister's cheek. "Hey, I'm going to class today okay, see you later?" She nodded, forcing a small smile.

"Later Tristan."

"Call if anything goes wrong, and keep an eye on Mom," he said as he opened the front door.

"Okay boss," she replied, making him smile before he exited. With a sigh, she got up, deciding to prepare something to eat in the kitchen to soothe her rumbling stomach. She took her plate of microwaved food and looked into the room at her mom who was still staring into space, before heading into her room. She felt a pang of pity and sadness thinking about her mother's condition.

******

Shawn leaned against his office chair, fiddling with the ball pen within his grasp. He stared at the ceiling, trying to figure out his next move. Diana had gone to the lab to get the results of David's autopsy, leaving him in the office to go through the rest of the evidence they'd gathered so far.

He let out a deep sigh, his mind consumed with multiple scenarios. Just then, the silence was interrupted by the shrill of the telephone ringing. He picked up the receiver, his curiosity piqued by the unfamiliar number.

"Detective Parker speaking," he answered in a diplomatic voice, as he was unsure of who was on the other side of the line. A trembling voice on the other end reached his ears. "Shawn, it's Victoria."

His eyes widened when he registered. "Victoria Hartfield?"

"Yes, I can't keep quiet anymore. I want to confess," she said, her voice no louder than a whisper. Shawn was a bit perplexed as to how the woman had suddenly recovered from her depression but made a mental note to bring it up later. For now, there were bigger issues on the ground.

"What is it? What's wrong?" He asked, sitting on the edge of his chair.

"I'm scared, and I need to confess. I can't keep this sin with me any longer," she said, her voice quivering. "I can't talk now. I'd rather tell you in person, meet me at the city park immediately. I'll be on my way there."

The call dropped.

"Hello? Hello!? Victoria?" He slammed the handset against the handset test and jumped to his feet. His heart throbbed as a sense of urgency washed over him. He recognized the desperation in Victoria's voice, the weight of her words. He knew he had to act swiftly. "Victoria, stay calm. I'm on my way. Just hold on," he muttered to himself, hoping the universe would carry his words to the heavens and present them as a small prayer.

He leaped into action, rushing out of his office with his car keys already in hand. With skillful maneuvering, he swerved through the traffic, missing fatal collisions with other vehicles by mere inches. He was hitting dangerous speeds but he just hoped that Victoria would be exactly where she said she'd be.

He slipped out his phone and tried to call Diana, but she wasn't picking up. He was sent to voicemail. "Look Diana, I'm on my way to the city park. Victoria called me and she was terrified. She said she had something to tell me. Call me immediately you receive this voicemail."

The park came into view, and he parked his car hastily, not minding that he was facing the road. He alighted, slamming his door closed as his eyes scanned the surroundings for any sign of Victoria. His heart pounded in his chest, the anticipation of the unknown fueling his steps.

As he moved through the park, his eyes darted from person to person, searching for the woman who had reached out to him in her time of fear. Finally, he spotted her, a figure standing at a distance, her body tense and her face etched with worry.

He called out her name as he rushed towards her, his long strides closing the distance between them.

Victoria turned around slowly, making her way towards the detective. Her gaze was firm.

But when the two were just a few inches away from each other, Victoria's body suddenly grew limp, her eyes rolled into her skull as her legs wobbled, and she slumped onto the floor, her body twitching. Shawn paused, lowering his body as he swiveled his head around in search of any threat.

He crouched beside Victoria. "Victoria? Victoria!" He called as he tapped her cheeks. He instinctively pressed his ears against her chest, then put fingers in front of her nostrils.

"No..." he muttered, realizing that she was dead. He looked around at all the suspicious faces of the onlookers, his eyes darting between them and trying to come to a conclusion. He closed her soulless eyes and laid her down on the grass.

Shawn felt a new type of rage bubbling within him when he realized that Victoria probably held the answer to who the killer was and she was killed right under his nose.

******

Dr. Philip stood in the autopsy room, his eyes fixed on the report in his hands. The air was thick with tension as he prepared to deliver the devastating news to Shawn and the grieving twins. The detectives had let the twins be present in this. After all, it was their mother who died, and they had the right to know.

Taking a deep breath, Philip retrieved the report from a file, ready to read it.

With a grave expression, Dr. Philip began, his voice steady but filled with empathy. "I've completed the autopsy on Victoria. It appears that she was poisoned with arsenic."

Tristan's eyes widened, shock and disbelief etched on his face. Taylor's hands instinctively flew to her mouth as tears welled up in her eyes. The revelation pierced their hearts, shattering their emotions. They could only imagine what their mother went through in her dying moments.

Shawn, determined to find answers, approached the devastated twins, his voice gentle but probing. "Tristan, can you tell me where you were during the time Victoria was poisoned?"

Tristan's voice shook with emotion as he responded, his eyes filled with pain. "I was at school. I was in class the entire time."

Shawn turned to Taylor, his tone compassionate yet insistent. "And what about you, Taylor? Where were you?"

Taylor's voice quivered as she spoke, her voice barely above a whisper. "I was in my room. Mom told me she was going out, but she didn't eat anything so I don't understand how she got poisoned."

"Maybe she ate something on the way?" Diana proposed. Shawn nodded, taking mental notes of their responses. He could see the devastation in their eyes, the raw grief that consumed them. But he couldn't ignore the nagging feeling at the back of his mind—a feeling that there was more to the story.

Returning to the office, frustration gripped Shawn, his thoughts spinning as he tried to make sense of the pieces that didn't fit. Diana approached, her voice calm and steady. "Shawn, take a moment to breathe. We'll find the answers, but we need to approach this with a clear mind."

Shawn paced the room, his frustration mounting. Suddenly, a realization struck him, a flicker of understanding in his eyes. He grabbed his blazer, the urgency pulsing through his veins. "Diana, I just realized something. I need to check on something immediately. I'll be back soon."

Without waiting for a response, Shawn hurriedly left the office, leaving a perplexed Diana behind. His mind raced, connecting the dots, as a new lead emerged—an inkling that his conversation with Victoria may have been overheard. Maybe their phones were already bugged.

As he rushed to his car, Shawn couldn't shake the feeling that time was slipping away.

******

Diana made her way towards Victoria's house with a small smile on her face. She and her partner had figured out who the killer was. She rang the doorbell, waiting for someone to get the door.

The door swung open, revealing Taylor's frame standing behind it, her eyes swollen and red from crying. "May I come in?" 'she asked. Taylor nodded, stepping aside for the detective.

Tristan was seated on the couch, with Natalie by his side, comforting him. "Once again my sincere condolences to the two of you. It must be tough going through what you're going through right now. I'll know because I've lost my mother before."

Tristan looked up at her, his eyes red and puffy. "I know who your mother's killer is," she said. The statement caused everyone in the room to sit upright, fixing their gazes on her in expectation. "For now, it's still classified information, but we're making plans to arrest the person within the next 24 hours."

"Who did it?" Tristan broke in.

"Why can't you tell us who it is?" Taylor asked, her voice shaky.

"Because I suspect that your devices have been bugged, or maybe even the house. And until we rectify that issue, I can't go about divulging this information to you guys. I've not even told Shawn about this. But I really feel sorry for you two and I wanted you guys to know that justice will be served for your mother."

The twins hugged each other, biting their lips to hold back sobs. "Okay, I'll be going home now. I'll see you guys later."

With that, she made her way into the streets, walking towards the subway. Diana couldn't shake off the feeling that she was being trailed.

Diana stepped into her house, her senses heightened as she made her way to her desk. She needed to gather the files. Her mind was focused on the case that had taken a dangerous turn. Suddenly, the sound of footsteps approaching reached her ears, causing her heart to race. Instinctively, she reached for her gun, ready to defend herself.

But before she could react, a swift blow struck her, sending her crashing against the floor. Pain shot through her body, momentarily disorienting her. As she struggled to regain her bearings, she turned her head, her eyes widening in alarm.

A masked figure stood before her, holding a syringe. Fear surged through Diana's veins as she realized the danger she was in. With adrenaline coursing through her, she fought back, using every ounce of strength to defend herself against the assailant.

The attacker swung weakly, giving her just enough time to dodge the blow. It was as if he was hesitant. She rammed her knee into his torso, reveling in a short-lived victory before she was taken off her feet and slammed against the wall. He reached for a flower vase, ready to mar her with it.

She looked up at the killer, chest heaving. Just then, Shawn burst into the room, the edge of his pistol hammering against the base of the assailant's neck, causing him to stagger.

Diana seized the opportunity to disarm the attacker and retrieve the syringe. "Took you long enough," she said to Shawn.

"Let's find out who this bad boy is," Shawn said with a hint of humor in his tone. As he pulled off the mask. Diana's eyes widened.

"Tristan?" She mouthed.

****

Diana knocked on the door and Natalie opened it, arching her eyebrows as she stepped aside to let them in. Taylor raised her head, shock enveloping her.

"Have you arrested the killer? Can you finally tell us who killed our mom?"

They shared a look before Shawn stepped forward. "It's Tristan."

"What?!" The girls both screamed in unison. Natalie shook her head slowly.

"You can't just arrest him because he came late to class that one time!'

Taylor shot her head towards Natalie, wondering what she was talking about.

"Look Natalie, I know it's a lot to take in, but you confirmed he came late to class. Why else would he come late if he didn't stay back to poison his mother when she was about to tell us he was the killer?" Diana pointed out.

"He asked you questions and you didn't even mention it even once!? Whose side are you on Natalie?" Taylor shot, feeling pity for her brother.

"I'm not on any side. I didn't have anything to hide because Tristan is innocent!"

41

"Really? Then why did you lie about him being in your place the night Jefferson was murdered?" Shawn asked, with arms folded against his chest. Her face fell, twitching as she struggled to maintain composure.

"H- how did you-"

"Tristan was home the entire time. The cops came to the house really early. There's no way he'd have left your house and gotten here before the cops arrived and opened the door for them in PJs. Plus, the CCTV cameras on the traffic lights by the corner didn't even pick any image of a taxi dropping Tristan off in the early hours of the morning on that day," Shawn explained.

She fell silent, lowering her head. Shawn continued. "Victoria was scared and she was killed way too fast. It had to be somebody within close proximity to her, and who better to poison her than a chemistry major living in her house?"

Taylor shook her head, "Tristan is innocent. He's innocent!"

"No, he's not. I've had my suspicions but the recent events have only confirmed it."

"Where's my brother?"

"At the station."

Chapter 5

Tristan was seated in the interrogation room, hands bound behind him and his head low. Shawn walked into the room, his face stern. He took his seat opposite Tristan, a small wooden table being the only thing that separated them.

He leaned onto the table, his fingers interlocking as he sighed. Diana walked into the room, grabbed a chair, and brought it near the table. She slouched her back against the seat, eyes fixed on Tristan. The detectives shared a look, and with a subtle nod or approval from Diana, Shawn began the investigation. "Why did you kill Jefferson?"

Tristan clenched his jaws, weighing his options.

"Don't even bother lying because we know-"

"I killed him," he blurted, interjecting Diana. "I killed him because he used to beat my mother up. I came back home that day to find my mother covered in bruises, which wasn't the first time he'd beat her up. She was too weak to leave him, so I... so I killed him."

"What about David? Why'd you kill him?" Diana asked.

"He used to hit Taylor. I hate those scumbags."

"So, you just went about killing all the abusive men in your lives. Then why did you kill Victoria? Why?"

Tears welled in Tristan's eyes when they mentioned his mother's death. "I panicked. I didn't want to get caught."

Flashback

Victoria's heart raced as strange noises echoed through the stillness of the night. Fear gripped her, and she instinctively crept towards her bedroom door, trying to discern the source of the disturbance. Her mind raced with worry, wondering what could be happening within the walls of her own home.

As she peered through the crack of her slightly ajar door, a chilling sight unfolded before her eyes. Tristan, her own son, was tiptoeing into the house, a bloody shirt clutched tightly in his hands. Shock and disbelief flooded Victoria as she struggled to comprehend the scene unfolding before her.

Her breath caught in her throat. She stood frozen for a moment, trying to process the unimaginable. It wasn't until in the morning when the police came over and confirmed Jeffersons's death, that the pieces of the puzzle fitted and she went into shock.

End of flashback

"When I was leaving for school that morning, I overheard her making a call with Shawn. I knew I had to stop her before she told him anything," he finished.

Diana scoffed, "I can't believe this, your mother."

"He's lying," Shawn deadpanned.

Diana turned to face him with an arched eyebrow. "The search warrant was approved yesterday, and the search team went to Victoria's house this morning. They found a bottle of the same kind of poison that killed Victoria hidden among Taylor's things. Taylor's in the other interrogation room as we speak."

Tristan jerked against his seat, trying to get up. "Leave her alone, she's innocent! I killed everyone. I did it," he cried, his protective instincts overshadowing his better judgment.

Taking a deep breath, Shawn began, his voice steady. "I have been investigating Taylor's involvement in these crimes, and the evidence points towards her as the real killer."

His eyes shifted between Diana and Tristan before he continued, his voice gentle but firm. "Taylor never spoke about the abuse she suffered at the hands of David until after his death. It seems that she had been carrying this secret burden alone. And the evidence, the bank transactions, they tell a damning story."

"We monitored Taylor's bank transactions, and it revealed that on the day Jefferson was murdered, she purchased a meat mallet from a nearby supermarket. And on the day David was killed, she bought a hammer. It appears that these acts were premeditated."

"So, when you told us you were going to arrest the criminal in 24 hours, it was a bait to lure her out into doing something," Tristan remarked.

Diana nodded, "what I don't understand is why you came to attack me with anesthetics."

Flashback

Her heart thundered within her chest like a wild stallion galloping in a race against time. She fixed her gaze upon the lifeless body sprawled before her, its complexion slowly losing its warmth. She had just killed Jefferson.

Each breath she drew felt like inhaling shards of ice, piercing her lungs with a frigid ache, as she fought to steady the tempest within.

An icy shiver slithered down her spine, sending a symphony of goosebumps dancing upon her flesh. Her trembling hands clung loosely to the blood-stained meat mallet, its weight both weapon and burden as if it held the weight of her unraveling soul. Her legs quivered, betraying her in this moment of despair, rendering her weak and helpless upon her knees.

Slowly, she dropped the meat mallet on the ground to avoid making any sound. Her teary eyes were still fixated on the body that lay on the ground.

The face of the body could hardly be recognized as it was bloody and disfigured by the many hammering it had gotten from the meat mallet.

The figure that now cowered over the dead body stood still. Initially devastated, her expression slowly transformed. She had committed a heinous act, taking the life of someone very close to her mother.

Panic consumed her, and she hastily rose to her feet, scanning the dimly lit alleyway for any signs of witnesses. Seeing no one in sight, she took to her heels and dashed into the darkness of the night, hoping to outrun the reality of what had just happened.

When she got home, the voices in her head began to taunt her as her emotions threatened to consume her. She slipped out her phone and called the only person she could trust at that moment, her brother Tristan.

Tristan came out to find her sobbing on the floor, her knees cradled against her chest. She confessed to murdering Jefferson Crawford. He immediately suggested that she remove the bloody shirt and that he was going to dispose of it. She entered through the front door and he entered through the back to get the lighter from the kitchen. That's when Victoria saw him.

****

That morning, just as Tristan stepped out to go to school, Taylor went to the kitchen to fix herself a snack. She overheard Victoria praying in her room; she was confessing her sins to a portrait of Mary in front of her. Taylor overheard her saying she couldn't hide what she saw that day any longer. Victoria thought Tristan was the killer.

Tristan stepped back in to find Taylor looking distraught. "I forgot my bus pass," he mouthed as he entered the house. The sound of the shower running met his ears. "Is someone taking a shower?"

Taylor nodded, "it's mum."

His eyes widened. "She's out of her depression?"

"I don't think she was ever depressed. She just played mute to avoid talking to the police. Mum thinks you're the one who killed Jefferson. She wants to tell Shawn about it."

Dread filled his chest as he ran his fingers through his hair. "Relax, I'll explain everything to her and talk to her about it.

You just go to school like usual, please?" He was hesitant but obliged.

Taylor then poisoned her mother's coffee and walked into the room, "Mom, you're fine now?" She asked, feigning surprise.

Victoria swallowed, "I'm sorry for not telling you honey, but I've just been quiet to avoid telling the cops something. I can't hold it in anymore; it's eating me up from the inside. Your brother killed Jefferson."

She gasped, covering her mouth with her palm. Victoria nodded, "I have to do the right thing and confess."

Taylor handed her the coffee. "Please drink up mom. I'll come with you."

Victoria smiled at her daughter's kind gesture, downing the content of the cup. "No honey, I'm in a rush. I have to leave now." And with that, Victoria left.

*****

"Why did you poison mom!? You said you wanted to talk to her!"

"It was the only way!" She screamed, her voice muffled with tears.

"What is wrong with you!?" He screamed, his eyes reddening.

Amidst the heated exchange, a sudden interruption broke through their bitter words. The doorbell rang, its chime slicing through the tension like a knife. Taylor, her face etched with anger and sadness, moved to answer the door.

As she swung the door open, Diana stood on the other side.

End of flashback

Mark Jenkins

"Of course, that's when Tristan decided to attack me because he thought he was trying to protect Taylor from being arrested."

"I couldn't bring myself to kill you. I thought I could just sedate you and take you somewhere."

Diana chuckled. "For how long? Do you really think you could kidnap me and get away with it, even if you successfully sedated me? You, young man, are in a lot of trouble."

A few months later

In the sterile halls of the mental institution, anticipation hung in the air as Tristan waited to be granted permission to see his sister. Taylor was found guilty of all three murders and she was confirmed to have psychotic disorders along with PTSD from having witnessed Lucas abuse her mother throughout her childhood before their divorce. This has set her on edge, causing her to go on a killing spree, attacking primarily the abusers in her life. Her sentence was a bit lenient.

She would spend the rest of her days within the confines of this hospital, bound to her bed with handcuffs and ropes. Tristan was let off the hook by the detectives. Regardless of his actions, they understood his bond with his twin sister and the naivety of it.

49

"Sir, you may come in to see the patient," the nurse said before entering back into the room. He and Natalie shared a look before entering.

Taylor was mute, most likely due to the effects of the antidepressants she was on. Tears welled in his eyes when he took in her vegetative state. They spent some time together, talking to Taylor since the doctor said it was good for her mental health.

Natalie's baby bump was already visible, and she shared her plans as well as baby names with Taylor. As they prepared to leave, Tristan promised to never turn his back on Taylor. He'd be there for her no matter what.

Printed in Dunstable, United Kingdom

71977997R00037